A to Z of
Ps and Qs

Written by Tracy Nelson Maurer

Photos by Linda Dingman, Diane Farleo, Julie Johanik,
Lois M. Nelson, Richele Bartkowiak, and Michelle Williams

Frog Street Press
www.frogstreet.com

About the Author:

Tracy Nelson Maurer specializes in nonfiction and business writing. Her most recently published children's books include the Green Thumb Guides series, published by Rourke Book Company. A University of Minnesota graduate, Tracy lives with her husband Mike and two children in Superior, Wisconsin.

PHOTO CREDITS:
© Photodisc, cover; © Linda Dingman, page 13, 16, 22, 26; © Diane Farleo, 6, 40, 48; © Julie Johanik, page 20, 25; © Lois M. Nelson, page 4, 8, 10, 12, 14, 18, 24, 28, 30, 32, 34, 26, 38, 42, 44, 46; Richele Bartkowiak, page 4, 25, 37, 40; © Michelle Williams, page 36.

Acknowledgments:
With appreciation to Margaret and Thomas for their joyful assistance in developing this series, and to Lois M. Nelson for her editing and enthusiastic support.

Library of Congress Catalog-In-Publication Data

Maurer, Tracy, 1965–
   A to Z of Ps and Qs / Tracy Nelson Maurer.
         p. cm. — (A to Z)
   ISBN 978-1-63237-327-4
      1. Conduct of life—Juvenile literature. [1.
Etiquette. 2. Conduct of life. 3. Alphabet.] I. Title

BJ1631 .M373 2001
395.1'22[E]—dc21   2001018589

Ps and Qs—Life's Magic Words

Long ago in England, people said, "Mind your pints and quarts." This meant to watch your drinking glasses at the table. Over time the phrase shortened to "Ps and Qs," but the meaning grew. Now Ps and Qs mean the "magic words" and actions of good manners. Follow the alphabet for ideas about polite things you can do.

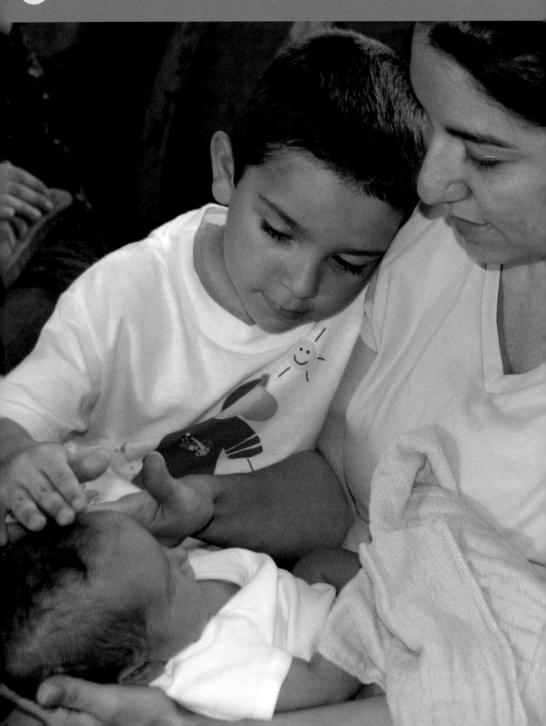

Ask your mom about her day.

Bb

Bring back what you borrow.

Cover your mouth to cough.

Dd

Drop your tissue in the trash.

Ee

Eat slowly and chew your food.

Ff

Fix it if you tear it.

Greet your friends.

15

Hh

Hold the snack for guests.

Invite the new boy to play.

Join the fun!

Kk

Keep still while mom helps you.

L l

Listen to the teacher.

Mail a thank-you note soon.

Nn

Notice when friends need help.

Open the card first.

Pp

"Pass the strawberries, please!"

A B C D E F G H I J K L M

Quietly wait your turn.

A B C D E F G H I J K L M

Rr

Right your wrongs.

Ss

Say "thank you" for the treats.

Tt

Tell the truth.

Uu

Use your napkin.

A B C D E F G H I J K L M

Vv

Visit with your grandpa.

Watch out for your little brother.

Xx

Excuse yourself from the table.

Yy

Yawn behind your hand.

Zz

Zap an e-mail to a friend.